KT-393-454

It's time for action.
COWS IN ACTION!

Genius cow Professor McMoo and
his trusty sidekicks, Pat and Bo,
are star agents of the C.I.A.
– short for COWS IN ACTION!
They travel through time, fighting evil
bulls from the future and keeping
history on the right track . . .

Find out more at
www.**cows**inaction.com

www.**kids**atrandomhouse.co.uk

www.cowsinaction.com

Read all the adventures of
McMoo, Pat and Bo:

THE TER-MOO-NATORS
THE MOO-MY'S CURSE
THE ROMAN MOO-STERY
THE WILD WEST MOO-NSTER
WORLD WAR MOO

also by Steve Cole:

ASTROSAURS

Riddle of the Raptors
The Hatching Horror
The Seas of Doom
The Mind-Swap Menace
The Skies of Fear
The Space Ghosts
Day of the Dino-Droids
The Terror-Bird Trap
The Planet of Peril
Teeth of the T. rex
(specially published for WBD)
The Star Pirates
The Claws of Christmas
The Sun-Snatchers
Revenge of the FANG

ASTROSAURS ACADEMY

Destination: Danger!
Contest Carnage!
Terror Underground!

www.stevecolebooks.co.uk

THE BATTLE FOR CHRISTMOOS

Steve Cole

Illustrated by Woody Fox

RED FOX

THE BATTLE FOR CHRISTMOOS
A RED FOX BOOK 978 1 862 30539 7

First published in Great Britain by Red Fox,
an imprint of Random House Children's Books
A Random House Group Company

This edition published 2008

1 3 5 7 9 10 8 6 4 2

Text copyright © Steve Cole, 2008
Illustrations copyright © Woody Fox, 2008

The right of Steve Cole to be identified as the author of this work has been
asserted in accordance with the Copyright, Designs and Patents Act 1988.

All rights reserved. No part of this publication may be reproduced, stored in
a retrieval system, or transmitted in any form or by any means, electronic,
mechanical, photocopying, recording or otherwise, without the prior
permission of the publishers.

The Random House Group Limited supports The Forest Stewardship
Council (FSC), the leading international forest certification organisation.
All our titles that are printed on Greenpeace approved FSC certified paper
carry the FSC logo. Our paper procurement policy can be found at
www.rbooks.co.uk/environment

Set in Bembo Schoolbook

Red Fox Books are published by Random House Children's Books,
61–63 Uxbridge Road, London W5 5SA

www.**kids**at**randomhouse**.co.uk
www.**rbooks**.co.uk
Addresses for companies within
The Random House Group Limited can be found at:
www.randomhouse.co.uk/offices.htm

THE RANDOM HOUSE GROUP Limited Reg. No. 954009

A CIP catalogue record for this book is available from the British Library.

Printed in the UK by CPI Bookmarque, Croydon, CR0 4TD

To Jack and Ethan O'Meara

★ THE C.I.A. FILES ★

Cows from the present —
Fighting in the past to protect the future . . .

In the year 2550, after thousands of years of being eaten and milked, cows finally live as equals with humans in their own country of Luckyburger. But a group of evil war-loving bulls — the Fed-up Bull Institute — is not satisfied.

Using time machines and deadly ter-moo-nator agents, the F.B.I. is trying to change Earth's history. These bulls plan to enslave all humans and put savage cows in charge of the planet. Their actions threaten to plunge all cowkind into cruel and cowardly chaos . . .

The C.I.A. was set up to stop them.

However, the best agents come not from 2550 — but from the past. From a time in the early 21st century, when the first clever cows began to appear. A time when a brainy bull named Angus McMoo invented the first time machine, little realizing he would soon become the F.B.I.'s number one enemy . . .

COWS OF COURAGE — TOP SECRET FILES

PROFESSOR ANGUS MCMOO

Security rating: Bravo Moo Zero

Stand-out features: Large white squares on coat, outstanding horns

Character: Scatterbrained, inventive, plucky and keen

Likes: Hot tea, history books, gadgets

Hates: Injustice, suffering, poor-quality tea bags

Ambition: To invent the electric sundial

LITTLE BO VINE

Security rating: For your cow pies only

Stand-out features: Luminous udder (colour varies)

Character: Tough, cheeky, ready-for-anything rebel

Likes: Fashion, chewing gum, self-defence classes

Hates: Bessie Barmer: the farmer's wife

Ambition: To run her own martial arts club for farmyard animals

PAT VINE

Security rating: Licence to fill (stomach with grass)

Stand-out features: Zigzags on coat

Character: Brave, loyal and practical

Likes: Solving problems, anything Professor McMoo does

Hates: Flies not easily swished by his tail

Ambition: To find a five-leaf clover — and to survive his dangerous missions!

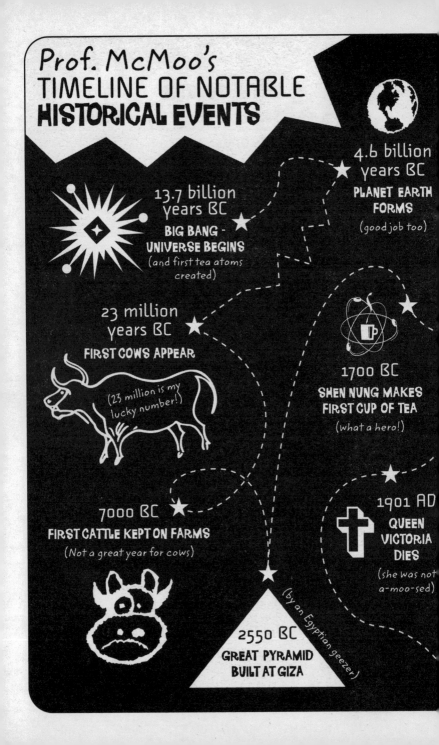

31 BC ROMAN EMPIRE FOUNDED

(Roam-Moo empire founded by a cow but no one remembers that)

1509 AD HENRY VIII COMES TO THE THRONE

(and probably squashes it)

1066 AD BATTLE OF HASTINGS

(but what about the Cattle of Hastings?)

1620 AD ENGLISH PILGRIMS SETTLE IN AMERICA

(bringing with them the first cows to moo in an American accent)

1939 AD WORLD WAR TWO BEGINS

(or World War Moo as it is known to cows)

2007 AD I INVENT A TIME MACHINE!!!

2500 AD COW NATION OF LUCKYBURGER FOUNDED

(HOORAY!)

(about time!)

1903 AD FIRST TEABAGS INVENTED

2550 AD COWS IN ACTION RECRUIT PROFESSOR McMOO, PAT AND BO

(and now the fun REALLY starts...)

THE BATTLE FOR CHRISTMOOS

Chapter One

THE PRESENT OF DOOM

Very few cows wear Santa hats, and none at all are known to put up Christmas decorations. But on the day before Christmas Eve, inside a tatty old shed on Farmer Barmer's organic farm, two cows were wearing Santa hats, putting up decorations *and* singing carols at the same time.

One was Pat Vine, a young bullock. The other was his big sister, a milk-cow called Little Bo Vine.

Untangling his home-made paper chains, Pat sang a festive farmyard carol: *"Oh, little coop of Beth the Hen! How still we see thee lie . . ."*

Bo took up the tune as she stuck tinsel

3

to the barn walls with chewed bubble gum: *"I just sat on some holly and it brought a tear to my eye . . ."*

"Those aren't the words!" Pat protested.

"The real words are boring!" Bo snorted. "Anyway, I prefer something with a killer bass line."

Pat sighed. He and Bo were both Emmsy-Squares, a very rare breed of clever cattle. But while Pat was quiet, thoughtful and liked to do things properly, Bo's life was a furious frenzy of fashion, fighting and painting her udder strange colours (today it was berry red). However, they did have one other thing in common . . .

They were both star agents in the C.I.A. – short for Cows in Action! – a crack team of commando cows from the twenty-sixth century.

The C.I.A. were a kind of time police, whose job was to stop anyone trying to change the past. As a result, although Pat and Bo lived in the twenty-first century, they had adventures all through history. And the shed they were decorating was no ordinary shed. It was their transport . . .

The first ever time machine!

"Hello, you two!" A large beaming bull barged through the barn's double doors. His coat was red and white, a pair of glasses was perched on his nose and he was waggling a piece of wire in one hoof. "Sorry I'm late," he went on,

"but the weather's so cold, it took me longer than usual to pick the lock on the main farm-gate."

Pat grinned to see the brilliant, brash (and very slightly bananas) Professor Angus McMoo. "Welcome back, Professor!" McMoo was an Emmsy-Square too — astoundingly clever, and Pat's all-time hero. "Where have you been?"

McMoo clapped his hooves together for warmth. "I was out posting our letters to Farmer Christmoos."

"Ah! Just think," said Pat happily. "Every Christmas Eve that jolly red bull flies through the night sky, on top of a big barn pulled by turkeys, delivering presents to farm animals all over the world!"

Suddenly, a jaunty jingling noise rang out.

Bo gasped. "That's not him now, is it?"

"Nope." McMoo kicked aside a hay

bale to reveal a big bronze lever in the wall. "It's the C.I.A. festive hotline. We're picking up a Christmas message from the twenty-sixth century – let's hear it!"

Pat's stomach tingled with excitement as McMoo yanked hard on the lever and a rattling, clanking sound started up. Tinsel twitched and hidden panels in the walls spun round to reveal reams of dials and switches. Cables wormed out of the woodwork like rubber snakes, pumping power into the horseshoe-shaped bank of controls sliding up from the ground. A computer screen swung down from the rafters and a large wardrobe, stuffed full of clothes from all times and places, popped into view by the far wall. In a matter of moments the lowly cattle shed had turned into an incredible control room, and the image of a big, tough, black bull appeared on the computer screen.

"Merry Christmoos, Yak!" cried McMoo. "How's the Director of the C.I.A. today?"

"Annoyed," growled Yak, holding up a dense tangle of wires and bulbs. "I'm supposed to be decorating C.I.A. headquarters. But I can't get these fairy lights to work, *and* my top electrical expert – Daisy Micklepud – has disappeared." He sighed. "I hope she's OK."

Bo blinked. "Why wouldn't she be?"

"Daisy was last seen working on a captured time machine," Yak began. "Some of my agents found it when we raided a secret F.B.I. base last Tuesday."

Pat caught his breath at the mention of the F.B.I. – short for Fed-up Bull Institute. They were a gang of bolshy bulls who wanted to change history for their own evil ends.

"We've always wanted to study one of the F.B.I.'s time machines," Yak went on. "Normally they self-destruct – but this one broke down before it could. Daisy was trying to get it working again – but nobody's seen her for two days."

Bo was wide-eyed. "Maybe it *did* self-destruct – and blew her to bits!"

"Or maybe Daisy just took it home to work on it there," said McMoo quickly, glaring at Bo. "Anyway, Yak, tell you what – why don't *I* fix your Christmas lights for you? The Time Shed can bring us to 2550 in no time at all!"

9

Yak smiled. "Thanks, Professor! Much obliged."

"Maybe we could stay for a bit," Pat piped up.

"Yeah, you can take me out clubbing, Yakky," said Bo. "We'll have a right laugh!"

"Great." Yak rolled his eyes. "See you soon, guys." And with that, the screen went blank.

"Looks like it really is the holiday season!" said McMoo happily.

Just then, a raucous, ratbag yell carried from across the field outside. "No, no, *NO*! You pea-brain, you've done it all wrong!"

Bo covered her ears. "Sounds like Bessie Barmer is on the warpath again."

"I shan't be sorry to leave *her* behind for a while!" said Pat with feeling. Bessie was Farmer Barmer's enormous wife. She had the body of a gorilla and the face of a gorilla's bottom. She hated all

10

the animals and couldn't wait to turn them all into pasties and pies.

"Honestly, a one-legged turkey with a dodgy beak would do a better job of hanging these decorations," Bessie's bellowing voice went on. "And I should know – my family have been expert Christmas decorators for centuries."

Bo tutted. "She's always going on about her amazing ancestors. As if anyone cares!"

"What do you mean, I said they were fine before?" Bessie raged on. "I was at the shops! I can't be in two places at once, can I?"

"I do hope not!" McMoo started darting about the shed, checking the controls. "Now, let's get ready to go. Goodbye, Farmer Barmer. Hello, future Christmas!" He paused and looked at Pat hopefully. "Just a quick cup of tea first, eh?"

Pat grinned and put the kettle on. The

professor was crazy about his cuppas,
and drank them by the bucketful. The
kettle soon came to the boil, but then—

BANG! BANG! BANG!

The shed doors rattled as someone
knocked on them loudly. The cattle
froze in alarm.

"Oh, no," hissed Pat. "What if it's
Bessie?"

"I can't turn the Time Shed back into
an ordinary shed when I'm this close to
take-off," McMoo whispered frantically.
"Bo, whoever's out there, get rid of
them."

Bo charged over to
the doors and flung
them open with a
loud *moo*. She trotted
outside . . . and moments
later came back in,
carrying a neatly
wrapped package
under one arm.

"Someone's left us a present!" she announced. "And the weird thing is, I saw Bessie marching away from the shed . . ."

"*Bessie?*" Pat shook his head in amazement. "But she hates us!"

"Who cares, I *love* pressies!" said Bo, ripping through the wrapping paper.

"Careful, Bo," McMoo warned her. "Perhaps I should take a look first—"

But it was too late.

Without warning, a sprig of holly burst out from the box like a dark-green bat. It zoomed around the Time Shed, its three berries glowing like evil eyes.

"What *is* that thing?" cried Pat.

Bo ducked as the holly-bat shot over

13

her head. "Someone's idea of a joke?"

McMoo dived out of its way. "Or an evil F.B.I. trap!"

"You mean you think that thing's been sent from the future?" Pat gulped. "But why?"

As he spoke, the holly-bat flew at the Time Shed's main power cable – and slashed straight through it with dagger-sharp wings.

"Pat. Bo. Get back!" The professor roared.

A massive explosion shook the shed, and the cows were sent tumbling. Pat stared in horror as vicious purple energy spat from the slashed wire. He grabbed hold of Bo's hoof as the Time Shed began to spin and splinter. Bales of hay caught fire, instrument panels erupted in sparks and levers started working by themselves.

"What's happening?" Bo shouted over the jerky whine of the shed's engines.

"Raw time power is flooding the shed!" McMoo stared helplessly at his melting instruments. "We're taking-off – for who knows where or when – completely out of control!"

Chapter Two

TRAPPED IN 1066

Pat choked on smoke as the Time Shed shook more and more fiercely. Dials exploded and switches shot about the room like bullets. "Professor," he shouted, "isn't there anything we can do?"

"We've got to stop our flight before the shed breaks apart!" McMoo galloped back over to the big lever in the wall. "If I can turn the Time Shed back into a cow shed it should cut the power . . ."

"But we're still travelling through time!" Pat protested. "Is it safe to change back?"

"Not remotely," McMoo admitted with a mad grin.

"Well it's not safe to stay flying either," Bo shouted. "Get on with it!"

"Right, hang on to your Santa hats!" McMoo grabbed the lever and pulled with all his might. A dreadful rasping, grinding noise started up. "Did it!"

"But not very well by the sound of things!" said Bo, covering her ears.

The panels in the wall were swinging back into place, but sparking wildly as they did so. The horseshoe of controls slid jerkily into the muddy ground. Piles of clothes burst out of the enormous wardrobe. Then the Time Shed turned

upside down and the C.I.A. agents were hurled into the decorated rafters. McMoo and Bo grabbed hold of some tinsel while Pat clung on to a string of fairy lights for dear life.

At last, with a sickening crunch of unseen gears, all the lights went out and the Time Shed turned the right way up again. McMoo, Pat and Bo dropped to the floor in an untidy sprawl.

"I'm glad I sent that letter to Farmer Christmoos asking for some lucky escapes this year!" said McMoo weakly.

"The flipping F.B.I.," Bo scowled. "Where do they get off, attacking us at Christmas?"

Pat let out a shaky breath. "I wonder where and when we've landed?"

"Let's take a peek," said McMoo.

Pat and Bo joined the professor as he cautiously opened the door. A gust of cold wind blew inside the smoky shed, and the three cows gulped

down the
fresh air. Then
they peered
outside ...
To find thirty
bearded men in
shabby trousers,
tunics and cloaks
– each holding a spear and a shield –
standing on a cold hillside, staring up at
them in total amazement!

"What are they looking at?" Bo
frowned. "Haven't they ever seen three
cows in a shed before?"

Pat looked down – and gasped. "I doubt they've ever seen three cows in a shed that's *floating ten metres above the ground*!"

The grubby-looking men yelled in fright, turned on their heels and ran away, babbling in a strange language.

McMoo looked thoughtful. "I think they were speaking old Anglo-Saxon . . ." He grinned at his two friends. "I *knew* that long-distance course I took in early-British languages would pay off some day!"

"What were they saying?" asked Pat.

McMoo cleared his throat. "Roughly translated . . .'Oooooh! Oh, dearie me! It's a secret weapon! Norman witchcraft! Flee for your lives from the invaders!'"

"Humans are weird," Bo declared. "How can a shed be a weapon? And who's Norman Witchcraft, anyway?"

"Not who, *what*," McMoo told her.

"The Normans were a bunch of people who lived in Normandy in northern France. They invaded England in 1066, led by William the Conqueror. Then they killed poor old King Harold at the Battle of Hastings, and managed to take over the country." He puffed out his cheeks and whistled. "Imagine that – the last successful invasion of England. What a turning point in history! What a—"

"Yeah, yeah," Bo interrupted. "Can't you stop us floating? I'm getting air-sick!"

"Sorry – the Time Shed's power gasses are lighter than air, and they must be leaking out through the floorboards into the atmosphere . . ." McMoo pulled a piece of chewed gum from behind Bo's ear, rushed over to the broken power cable and stuck the ends back together. "There!" The shed sank gently down towards the hillside. "That should slow the leak until the self-repair systems kick in." McMoo looked around at his burned-out barn and sighed. "But those systems run off the energy banks, and I'm afraid it will take some time for them to recharge."

Pat frowned. "And until then we're stuck in 1066?"

"We might as well make the best of it!" McMoo passed Pat and Bo a special silver nose ring each. "Pop in your ringblenders while I dig out some clothes from the wardrobe, then let's ask the natives exactly where we are."

Pat fixed the brilliant C.I.A. gadget to his nose. Any cow wearing a ringblender could pass themselves off as a human being – so long as they were wearing the right clothes. The clever gadgets also meant that cows and humans could understand each other, so C.I.A. agents could fit in as locals wherever and whenever they ended up.

"One day, you'll take us to a time that had funky fashion sense," Bo complained, squeezing into a long, linen slip, then pulling a blue woollen dress over the top.

"I don't think I look too bad," Pat declared. He was wearing pale-blue trousers and a brown tunic, with a wide leather belt around his waist. The professor put on a similar outfit, topped off with a long blue cloak that he fixed round his neck with a bronze brooch.

"Now then, where's the magic mirror gone?" asked McMoo, hunting about. "You know, the special C.I.A. one that shows us how we'll appear to human beings . . ."

"Here's some of it!" said Bo, pointing to a broken shard of glass on the ground.

They all looked down. Pat saw himself transformed in the mirror as a young, blond-haired lad, Bo as a flaxen-haired,

24

rosy-cheeked maiden and McMoo was a wise, lordly looking man with a red beard.

Pat felt uneasy. "Breaking a mirror is meant to bring seven years' bad luck."

"Superstitious nonsense!" McMoo retorted, carefully picking up the piece of mirror – just as an arrow whistled through the air and shattered it! "Um, probably . . ."

Pat whirled round to find two men in armour framed in the Time-Shed doorway. One sat astride a stocky stallion, holding a shield and a long spear. The other stood beside him, wielding a bow and arrow.

Slowly, silently, they advanced on the unarmed cattle . . .

Chapter Three

THE CHRISTMAS CAMP

McMoo grinned at the advancing soldiers. "Hello! How goes the day, my lords?"

The two men stopped and looked at each other. Then, the one on horseback removed his helmet to reveal a puzzled, clean-shaven face. "He speaks French as we do, Tostain!"

"So it would seem, Renouf," said Tostain, the man on foot. He took his own helmet off to reveal a chubbier face and stared at McMoo, Pat and Bo with small suspicious eyes. "Are you Norman, as we are?"

"Nah, his name is Angus," Bo began, but Pat quickly nudged her in the ribs.

26

"We're all Normans," said McMoo hastily. "I am Lord Angus of Burger, and my friends are Pat Partridge-Peartree and Bo of Bo-Jangles. Long live King William!"

"Our conquering lord is not king yet," said Renouf, the man on horseback. "William, Duke of Normandy, will be crowned on Christmas Day, two days from now."

"Hear that?" McMoo whispered to his friends. "It's 23rd December, 1066, and we're just in time for a medieval coronation." He grinned. "Imagine *that*! If I only had a cup of tea and a mince pie in my hooves, life would be complete . . ."

Pat noticed the Normans frown. "Er, Professor," he hissed. "Perhaps this isn't the best time to get over-excited!"

"How did the three of you get here?" Tostain demanded.

"Oh, we just sailed over from

Normandy, nipped up the Thames and landed in London a couple of days ago," said McMoo airily. "We didn't want to miss William's big moment."

Renouf looked thoughtful. "We rode out here today because we heard the Saxons planned to attack William's camp beyond the hills," he said. "But then we saw them running away screaming in terror about Norman witchcraft . . ."

"That was down to the professor – er, Angus," said Pat proudly.

Bo rolled her eyes. "Yes, he can be very scary."

"Then we owe you our thanks," said Tostain, smiling at last. "That band of surly Saxons is led by Ethelbad the 'Orrible – William's sworn enemy."

Renouf nodded. "William will wish to thank you in person. Please, Angus, allow us to take you and your friends to our camp."

"Wa-heyy!" cheered McMoo, nearly knocking the Normans over as he scrambled for the shed's doors. "Let's go!"

"What about the Time Shed?" Bo hissed.

McMoo ran back. "I've told you, we're stuck here till its energy banks recharge." He pulled out a device, covered in little dials and lights, from inside his tunic. "Luckily I've invented a long-range Time-Power Sensor – it will tell me when the Time Shed is ready to rock. And in the meantime, since we're not on a C.I.A. mission for once, we can enjoy being time-tourists!" He grinned at the Norman soldiers and dashed outside. "Up this hill, is it? Come on, don't dawdle!"

It was
quite a trek to
the conqueror's camp.
Renouf and Tostain – remembering
that they were the new arrivals' escorts,
not their followers – hurried on ahead.
It was bitterly cold, and Pat and Bo had
put their Santa hats back on for extra
warmth.

"Er, Professor," said Pat as they
trudged up the hill. "Why do you want
to meet William the Conqueror
anyway? He doesn't sound very nice,
killing kings and invading countries."

"The past is a bloodthirsty place,"
McMoo agreed. "But William believed
he had a true claim to the throne of
England. He made the country a lot
more organized. Many people found

themselves
better off than before."

"Well *we're* a lot *worse* off," said
Bo grumpily. "I was all set for a cool
future yule – I bet these Normans
don't even bother to celebrate
Christmas."

Pat gasped as they reached the top
of the hill. "I wouldn't be too sure about
that!"

McMoo and Bo stood beside him and
all three stared down in amazement. Pat
had been expecting a bunch of tents.

But there, nestling in a woodland clearing, was something that looked more like Santa's grotto!

Wooden posts had been placed around the camp, each one wrapped up in bushy golden tinsel. Large Christmas trees, with glittery baubles dangling from every branch, were dotted about and multicoloured fairy lights flashed and flickered on every tent.

"We must be dreaming," said Pat in a daze.

"Welcome to the duke's camp!" Renouf cried from his horse. "It is quite remarkable, no?"

Bo nodded. "I have to admit, as festive camps go, it's not bad."

"*Not bad*?" McMoo frowned. "It's terrible!"

"That's a bit harsh." Then Bo shrugged. "I mean, obviously they should also have a killer sound system pumping out Christmas hits, but—"

"They didn't have decorations like this a thousand years ago!" McMoo exploded. "How are these lights even working? There's no electricity in 1066, so how can there be electric bulbs?"

"Someone's messing about with time," Bo realized. "It must be the F.B.I. They tried to get rid of us with their booby trap – but instead we've turned up right on their doorstep. How lucky is that?"

"Too lucky," Pat muttered. "Perhaps they *brought* us here . . ."

Bo frowned. "Don't be dumb! They sent us whizzing off, out of control."

"And even if they hadn't, Yak would have sent us here soon anyway to muck up their plans – so why bother?" McMoo looked deep in thought. "It *is* a strange coincidence, Pat. But perhaps when I made the emergency stop, the shed locked on to the nearest disturbance in time . . ."

"Who cares how we got here?" Bo complained. "It's time we sorted things out – with a few hoof sandwiches!"

"Let's try asking a few questions first, shall we?" McMoo suggested, marching up to Tostain and Renouf. "Tell me, you two – Where did these decorations come from? And what's powering the lights?"

"These Christmas trinkets are the invention of a remarkable Saxon maid," Renouf informed him. "A fine

34

woman who wishes to aid us."

McMoo raised his eyebrows. "Well, I'd very much like to meet her."

"Behold," said Tostain, pointing to the camp gateway. "Here she comes now."

Pat stared in disbelief as an enormous woman wobbled out of the camp, carrying a small mountain of holly wreaths in her arms. She had hair like lank straw and piggy eyes the colour of poo. Her greasy, spotty face was so revolting it would make a dog sick – and it certainly had a big effect on the Cows in Action.

"I should've known," said McMoo.

"Oh, no!" Bo groaned. "It can't be . . ."

"But it is," said Pat, eyes wide. "It's one of Bessie Barmer's awful ancestors. *She* must be the one mucking about with time!"

Chapter Four

THE NORMAN COWQUEST

"Hey, you!" McMoo charged down into the clearing to confront the woman. "What's going on with these dire decorations? Where are your F.B.I. masters?"

"What are you on about?" The woman frowned. "I am Bettie Barmas, local wise woman and friend to all Normans."

"A likely story," McMoo snorted. She shrugged. "If I'm not their friend, how come I bothered to learn their Norman language?"

36

"It is true," said Renouf, who had galloped up to join them. "Bettie is loyal to our cause and has made these marvellous, magical decorations for us. William is giving them to the people of London free of charge, to show that we Normans are not so bad after all."

"That's right," said Bettie. "I invented these clever things myself."

"Oh yes? *How*?" McMoo grabbed a garland. "This isn't real holly, it's plastic – and the first plastic wasn't invented until the nineteenth century. Explain that!"

"I do not understand your words, strange sir!" Bettie protested. "Now, if you will excuse me, I must go. William has approved my beautiful wreaths, so I must deliver them on his behalf. How the people of London will praise his kindness and cleverness . . ."

"Indeed they will," said Renouf, bowing his head to her. "Go in peace."

With a glare at McMoo, Bettie bundled off towards the nearby woods with her mysterious decorations — just as Pat and Bo arrived with Tostain.

McMoo drew his friends to one side. "Pat, Bo. There's something seriously dodgy going on round here. I'll find out more here while you go after Bettie. Watch out for ter-moo-nators!"

Pat's tummy quivered at the thought. Ter-moo-nators were sinister F.B.I. agents — half-bull, half-robot, with super-sneaky computer minds. By dressing up and wearing ringblenders, they, like the C.I.A., could fool people into thinking they were human. But other cattle could see through the disguise . . . just as a ter-moo-nator would see through theirs.

"We'll be careful," he muttered.

"Right then!" Bo turned to Tostain and Renouf and blew them a kiss. "Just going for a quick walk in the woods.

Give our love to Willy the Conk. Bye!"
And before anyone could say another
word, she and Pat dashed away.

"Kids, eh?" said McMoo, smiling at his
Norman escorts. "Where *do* they get
their energy from?" He glanced up at
the twinkling fairy lights. "And where
do *they* get their energy from?"

Suddenly, a large man with thick red
hair strode out from a large tent, flanked
by burly guards. His features were as
fine and handsome as the clothes he
wore. Tostain and Renouf quickly
bowed down before him. "Your grace!"
they chorused.

McMoo gasped. "William the Conqueror!"

"Well, my lords?" William demanded. "Does Ethelbad plot to attack us with his Saxon rabble?"

"Indeed, that was his plan . . ." Tostain turned to McMoo. "But mighty Angus of Burger here scared him away! We saw Ethelbad's men flee in terror."

McMoo smiled modestly. "I suppose you could say we surprised them."

"England is full of surprises, Angus," said William, waving a hand at the tinsel and lights. "Have you ever seen such divine decorations?"

"Not lately," McMoo admitted. "But why would a warrior like you bother with a bunch of baubles?"

William flung his arms in the air. "Because I'm fed up of fighting all the time!" he cried. "I won the Battle of Hastings on the 14th October and since then it's been nothing but fights, scraps, tussles and massacres all the way to London. I'm sick of skewering Saxons! Bored with burning villages to prove I'm boss! Tired of attacking townspeople to show them who's the daddy!" He sighed and sank to the ground, looking worn out. "Quite frankly, after two and a half months, my conquering has lost its conk. So I thought I'd show them my nice side for a change."

Tostain nodded quickly. "Giving the Saxons such delightful Christmas gifts is a sure way to impress them, your grace."

"Knowing how kind you are, they will welcome you to the throne on Christmas Day," Renouf added.

William nodded. "But sadly, my pressies *haven't* won over that rotten rascal Ethelbad the 'Orrible. The swine wants to be king in my place. He will do anything in his power to stop me being crowned." The conqueror smiled suddenly, "Still, he won't dare attack me now, will he? Not with Angus around!"

McMoo frowned. "Eh?"

"If Ethelbad's army shows up, we'll simply send you out to scare them away again," said William. "Single-handed!"

"Well, I'm not sure I . . ." McMoo began. But he was quickly drowned out, first by the cheers of Renouf and Tostain, then the whoops of the nearby soldiers, and pretty soon the singing and dancing of the entire Norman camp.

"Oh, dear," sighed McMoo to himself. "I only hope I can solve the mystery of these out-of-time decorations before I run out of time myself!"

While McMoo tangled with royalty at the camp, Pat and Bo were tangled up in bracken – trailing Bettie Barmas through the dark forest. The Saxon woman crashed through the undergrowth with her pile of plastic wreaths until she finally emerged into the city.

But as the C.I.A. agents stepped out of the woods, they had to shield their eyes from the sudden glare. The noisy medieval street they stood in was completely covered with modern festive decorations!

Dazzling bulbs of every hue dangled overhead from tatty thatched roofs. Illuminated plastic candy canes hung from the rickety houses' wooden walls. As the sun sank, their merry glow lit the antics of Bettie Barmas as she handed out holly wreaths to everyone she passed. "Here you go!" she bellowed. "Another festive gift from William the Conqueror to celebrate his being crowned this Christmas. He wishes peace and joy to one and all!"

She waddled along, fatter than Santa but a lot less jolly. Beggars and traders, pickpockets and rubbish rakers, even herders steering pigs through the grimy streets took her wreaths with a happy smile. Many of them already wore tinsel around their waists as belts.

"This is crazy," said Pat, studying the decorations closely. "These strings of lights are all exactly the same, even down to scratch marks on the cord and certain bulbs not working."

Bo looked all around. "They don't seem to plug in anywhere either ..." She sighed. "Why would the F.B.I. bother putting up a load of Christmas stuff?"

"I don't know." Pat frowned. "Hey, where did Bettie go? She's vanished!"

"Maybe she ducked into one of these houses," said Bo. "Let's ask someone."

"Ask *me* if you like," came a deep voice right behind them.

Pat whirled round to find a huge burly man with dark staring eyes, a long blond beard and a very large axe. He wore a muddy helmet and a dirty suit made of sackcloth.  Twenty or so grubby men armed with sticks and daggers had gathered around him. With a sinking feeling, Pat recognized them as the same Saxons they had accidentally scared when the Time Shed arrived on the hillside.

"I'm Ethelbad the 'Orrible!" The big man smiled, showing a mouth full of broken teeth. "The sworn enemy of all Norman ninnies."

"Um, we're Saxons," said Pat, slapping a hoof over his sister's mouth before she could say something he might regret.

"Don't think so." Ethelbad guffawed. "My spies saw you walk out of that bewitched barn with two Norman lords, heading for William's camp!"

"Oh," Pat gulped. "We were just, er, sightseeing!"

"Hark my words, Norman scum," sneered Ethelbad. "I will be crowned king on Christmas Day – not your stupid Duke William!"

"I'm very happy for you," said Pat politely. "Still, my sister and I had better be going—"

"You'll be going, all right – headfirst!" Ethelbad glanced back at his band of bruisers. "Men, *get them!*"

Chapter Five

THE DOMAIN OF DANGER

Roaring and yelling, Ethelbad's men charged forward, sticks and spears raised to attack.

"Run!" Pat cried.

Bo sprinted towards the Saxon mob.

Pat groaned. "No, Bo, I meant run *away*!"

"Now you tell me!" said Bo, whacking two men in the stomach with her front hooves. She turned and tail-whipped another, then spun about and squirted three more with a milk-blast from her udder. But one bruiser pushed past the spluttering trio and landed a lucky blow to Bo's head. With a cry, she sank to the floor as four more men gathered around her, sticks in the air . . .

"Get away from her!" Pat shouted, dodging a spear and shunting another Saxon aside. "Bo, get up, quick!"

"Right you are!" Bo performed a perfect backflip and landed on her hooves, whacking two more Saxons aside as she did so. "Let's get out of here!"

But when they turned to run, Ethelbad jumped out to block their way. He was whirling a huge glowing net, made from several strings of Christmas lights, over his head – and moments later, the tangled web of multicoloured bulbs had covered Pat and Bo. The more they struggled to get free, the more trapped they became.

Ethelbad gave a grunt of satisfaction.

"Naughty, naughty, Normans," he rasped. "You've made me and my friends angry . . ."

"Use your head, Ethelbad," said Pat, fighting to stay calm. "We are close personal friends of William the Conqueror."

Bo frowned. "We are?"

"Of course we are," said Pat, winking at her. "I'm the famous Norman, Pat Partridge-Peartree, and this is Bo of Bo-Jangles. I bet if you tell our pal Willy that you're holding us prisoner, he'll do anything you ask."

The huge hairy Saxon stared down at them in silence. Then he turned back to his men, who were still picking themselves up from the ground. "All right, boys. Take these Norman ninnies back to our camp. And send word to William that his lordly chums are in my power. If he wants to keep them alive, he must send food and ale – and that's just for starters!"

Ethelbad's men laughed and cheered, and hauled Pat and Bo roughly away.

"Nice one, Pat," whispered Bo. "That was quick thinking."

Pat smiled weakly. "Hopefully the professor will hear we're in trouble and come to our rescue." Suddenly, he noticed Bettie Barmas, watching stony-faced from the window of one of the houses. With a thrill of fear, Pat thought he glimpsed a cow-like figure standing just behind her – and the flash of green eyes . . .

"Bo," he whispered. "I think I might have just seen a ter-moo-nator!"

As the first flakes of snow began to drift through the moonlit sky, Professor

McMoo paced up and down near the entrance to William's camp. The fairy lights cast a soft glow over the wintry scene – but McMoo was far too worried to feel festive.

Tostain poked his head out of a nearby tent. "All that stamping is keeping me awake, Angus! What's the matter?"

"My young friends should be back by now." McMoo sighed. "I hope they're all right."

"They seem hardy enough," remarked Tostain. "They probably just got tied up somewhere . . ."

Suddenly, an arrow shot past the professor's head. *Thunk!* It struck a wooden post, slicing a rope of tinsel in two.

"We're under attack!" cried Tostain. "Everyone up!" Within moments, Renouf arrived on horseback, followed by hordes of soldiers and William himself in a grotty green nightshirt.

"Hold your horse, Renouf!" cried McMoo. "And calm down, the rest of you. I don't think it's an attack." He unwrapped a piece of parchment from the shaft of the arrow and held it up. "It's a message." But he gasped as he read the Saxon scrawl. "You were right, Tostain. Pat and Bo *have* been tied up – by Ethelbad the 'Orrible! He demands a Christmas feast of five hundred barrels of ale, sixty loaves of

bread and two thousand Cornish pilchards be delivered to his domain on the other side of London, or else he will do something terrible to my friends!" McMoo turned to William with a hopeful smile. "You can spare that, right?"

"I? Give food and drink to that rascal? Certainly not!" William shook his head. "Besides, pilchards are my absolute favourite and I only have seventeen left!"

Tostain clapped the professor heartily on the back. "You know, Angus, this seems the perfect chance for you to scare that slimy Saxon right out of London."

"Oh, yes!" Renouf galloped up and gave McMoo an encouraging smile. "Go alone to Ethelbad and his band of savage, dangerously unhinged barbarian killers and show them that you won't stand for any nonsense!"

"Thanks for your support, fellas."
McMoo sighed, straightened his glasses,
then stalked off through the settling snow
towards the forest. "Well, I'd better be off."

William yelled after him, "No time like
the present, eh?"

"No time at all," McMoo muttered, as
he entered the dark forest. "And how I
wish I was there now – not stuck in
1066!"

Even in the dark, it didn't take the
professor long to find his way to
Ethelbad's camp. Bettie Barmas had
trampled a clear path through the forest,

and the London of 1066 was a lot
smaller than in McMoo's time – he
crossed it in just twenty minutes. But
the thrill of touring eleventh-century
London was spoiled for him by the
endless Christmas lights and decorations
strewn about the city. They left the
dingy, smelly, crooked streets neon-
bright.

An uneasy feeling filled McMoo's
stomach. Why was the Fed-up Bull
Institute bringing modern Christmas
decorations into the past? And with no
plugs or electricity in 1066, what energy

was making them work?

"Speaking of energy," McMoo murmured to himself, "I wonder how quickly the Time Shed's banks are recharging?" He pulled out the time-power gadget, checked the levels and sighed. "It's taking a lot longer than I thought it would . . ."

Suddenly, four large, threatening Saxons stepped out from an alley to block his way.

"Hello!" said McMoo brightly. "I'm looking for Ethelbad's camp."

A bald, bloated Saxon stood aside to reveal a large hole in a broken old fence. "You've just found it, Norman scum — but you'll soon wish you hadn't!"

The four men grabbed McMoo and bundled him away into the smelly, sweaty darkness of Ethelbad's domain . . .

Chapter Six

MENACE BY MOO-NLIGHT

McMoo found himself in a large yard that stank of wee and rotten meat despite the light carpeting of snow. Small shabby huts with patchy thatched roofs were arranged around a big, ramshackle hall. He could hear the splutter of Saxon snores and the squeal of rats gnawing on discarded bones – and then deep, rocking laughter from the main hall.

"Your boss in there, is he?" McMoo enquired.

The bald Saxon nodded. "Ethelbad is having a secret meeting."

"So, the special Christmas turkeys have been prepared!" The deep voice boomed from the hall like cannon-fire. "Excellent!"

"Hmm." McMoo raised his eyebrows at the bald Saxon. "At that volume it's not *terribly* secret is it?"

"Make sure these marvellous birds are handed out to all the noble families of London," Ethelbad went on in bellowing tones. "Our lordly neighbours must believe they are a wondrous gift from William, not to be cooked till Christmas Day . . ."

"Speaking of food, Ethelbad," the professor yelled, "I've come from William's camp in response to that sweet message you sent."

The hall fell silent for a moment. Then the ground shook with the sound of heavy footsteps, and a massive, misshapen figure in a metal war helmet appeared in the doorway. "Who dares interrupt the secret meeting of Ethelbad the 'Orrible?"

"Some people in Wales, complaining about the noise?" McMoo suggested. "Oh, and me, of course. Hello!" He smiled cheerily as more glowering Saxons emerged from their huts. "The name's McMoo. Who's your secret meeting with then?"

"Be silent." Ethelbad's eyes narrowed beneath his bushy brows. "You *have* brought the food and drink I demanded?"

"First," said McMoo firmly. "Show me my friends are all right."

Ethelbad nodded to three of his men,

who vanished into a hut and came out soon after, dragging two familiar figures in a net behind them.

"Pat! Bo!" McMoo beamed. "Are you all right?"

"We are now you're here!" Pat declared.

"Apart from being trussed up in a tangle of fairy lights," Bo complained. "Some of the bulbs are getting hot in *very* awkward places!"

"Shut up!" roared Ethelbad. "Now, McMoo – where's my food and ale?"

"I'm surprised you need more food when you've got all those special Christmas turkeys prepared in your camp," said McMoo. "Although turkey is a funny choice for Christmas dinner in 1066, isn't it? You Saxons celebrate with roast lark or goose or wild boar. Turkey at Christmas doesn't take off for another five hundred years. Henry the Eighth – he was the first to have it on Christmas Day. I've met him, you know . . ."

"Stop this babbling!" Ethelbad stamped towards him. "I demanded five hundred barrels of ale, sixty loaves, and two thousand pilchards. Where are they?"

"Sadly, William couldn't quite stretch to the full amount," McMoo admitted, turning out his pockets. "But I *did* find an acorn, a dead mackerel and a cooking apple on my way here." He held out his smelly offering to the Saxon chief. "Will they do?"

Bo groaned, and Pat held his hooves over his eyes.

Ethelbad's eye began to twitch. He opened his huge mouth to bellow in anger . . .

And McMoo shoved the cooking apple into it!

Gasping and spluttering, with a hard fruit jammed tightly between his teeth, Ethelbad staggered back – and the professor hurled his acorn at one of the three men guarding Pat and Bo. Like a mini-missile, the nut pinged off his head and struck the guard beside him! Both of them fell with a cry and crashed into the third.

Bo quickly reached through the net and grabbed a sword from one of the fallen men. "Come on, Pat, we're busting out!" she cried, and split the plastic net wide open.

"Nice one!" cried McMoo, running towards his friends. But Ethelbad's men were hard on his heels – so he dropped the slimy fish over his shoulder.

"Whoa!" The bald bruiser skidded in the rotten fish and fell backwards onto his butt. His friends couldn't stop in time and tripped over him, landing in the gooey mess too.

Bo smiled as she chucked the sword away and helped Pat to his feet. "At least they'll all smell a bit better now!"

"They'll smell *a lot* better when we're miles away," said McMoo, grabbing hold of his friends' hooves as he ran towards the camp's high fence. "Come on!"

But Ethelbad had finally spat out the giant apple and was sprinting after them with his axe. "You can't escape me!"

Pat lowered his head and charged the fence. The rotten wood splintered about him, and Bo and McMoo followed him through the hole and out into a slippery, snow-covered street.

"This way," said the professor, charging off again.

"Professor, wait!" Pat panted. "I think I saw a ter-moo-nator before, with Bettie Barmas, in a house close to where we were caught."

McMoo skidded to a halt and grabbed hold of Pat urgently. "Do you remember where?"

"Um . . . !" Pat stared round, trying to get his bearings in the glow of the lights. "I'm not sure!"

Suddenly, Ethelbad and his gang came into sight, pounding down the road towards them. "I think we came this way," said Bo, leading the way down a crooked alley. But seconds later, she came up short against a huge pile of rubbish and the back of another house. "Pants! It's a dead end!"

"Now then, my three fine Norman ninnies . . ." With a stab of dread, Pat saw that Ethelbad and his men were blocking their way back out. The Saxon chief raised his axe. "I *shall* send you back to William – in pieces!"

McMoo stood bravely in front of Pat and Bo as Ethelbad advanced towards them.

But suddenly, the Christmas lights dangling above them flickered and grew brighter, *brighter* – until the bulbs exploded! Blue sparks began to flicker about the dirty wooden alleyway and Pat felt the hairs on his coat stand on end.

Ethelbad stared round in alarm – then dropped his axe as a sizzle of power shot along the length of it. "What's this?" he demanded, terrified. "Witchcraft?"

"More like an electrostatic shock-beam," said McMoo, peering at the light show through his glasses. "But in 1066? It's unheard of!"

The other Saxons cried out too as more crackles of power shot up their trouser legs like electric ferrets. They turned and ran, and Ethelbad soon fled from the alleyway after them.

Then Pat gasped. The figure of a cow on two legs stepped into sight at the end of the alley. The shadowy shape walked towards them, green eyes agleam . . .

"P–P–Professor, that's the thing I saw before, in the window with Bettie," he gabbled. "The ter–moo–nator – it's found us!"

Chapter Seven

THE DAISY DILEMMA

"Me? A ter-moo-nator?" The cow gave gales of high-pitched laughter. "Don't be daft, chuck! I just saved you, didn't I?"

As clouds shifted from in front of the midnight moon, Pat saw the newcomer more clearly. He realized there was nothing robotic about this cow. Her pretty green eyes sparkled like the length of tinsel tied around her tail.

She wore a deep-blue sash over her black-and-white coat, a rumpled party hat on her head and had a Christmas bauble dangling from each ear. "I saw those nasty fellas catch you in the street and thought you might need some help," the cow went on. "Shame I had to overload that set of fairy lights with my electro-beam . . ." She held up the torch-like device she was carrying, then pulled out another string of flashing bulbs from under her sash. "But luckily I've got plenty spare!"

"So *you're* the one who's been making these modern Christmas decorations?" McMoo scratched his head. "But you're wearing a C.I.A. sash!"

"Course I am! And you're C.I.A. agents too. I saw through your ringblender disguises in a moment – Pat and Bo Vine, and dishy old Angus McMoo." The cow grinned and shook her tinselly tail. "I'm Daisy Micklepud, the C.I.A.'s top electrical expert – and I just *love* Christmas, whatever the year!"

"Hey, hang on . . ." Pat boggled at the newcomer. "You're the one Yak told us went missing!"

"After you'd been tinkering with an F.B.I. time machine," McMoo agreed gravely. "What's going on, Daisy? The C.I.A. was set up to stop people mucking around with time – but by putting up all these Christmas decorations that's exactly what you're doing!"

"Don't be cross with me, chuck!" Daisy's tail drooped. "Come back to Bettie Barmas's house and let me explain."

"You're friends with Bettie, then?" asked Pat.

Daisy nodded. "You could say we're helping each other out. Come on, lovies! This way!"

The four cows trotted quickly through the medieval maze of narrow streets. Daisy didn't have a ringblender, so Pat pretended he was herding her through the city. But the Christmas-mad cow couldn't stop singing carols, and Bo had to keep shushing her.

Finally, they made it to Bettie's home – though Bettie herself was not there. The wooden house was bare inside, save for a stool, a bench and a small log fire. The floor was packed earth and littered with straw – it reminded Pat of his bed back on the farm.

"Let's cheer the place up a bit," said Daisy, crossing to a curtain at the back of the room. Beyond it stood a cramped Christmas grotto with fairy lights flashing, a decorated tree in the corner and a workbench littered with futuristic tools. "There! Much better!"

McMoo sighed and sat down with Pat and Bo as Daisy began her strange story.

"So – there I was in my workshop," she explained, "trying to make that wretched broken F.B.I. time machine work . . . when suddenly, it switched itself on and whisked me back to 1066! There must have been a power surge, 'cos it dragged my workbench, my tools, even the workshop's Christmas decorations along with me – and then stopped working again! I woke up to find it was December 1st, 1066, and I was marooned in a cold forest with no way of calling for help, no protection and nowhere to go . . ." She used her paper hat as a tissue and dabbed delicately at the tears in her eyes. "Anyway, Bettie Barmas found me first. I gave her quite a shock, me being a clever cow with all my tools and flashy Christmas stuff. And I knew that if she ran off and told people, then cow technology from the twenty-sixth century would fall into the hands of eleventh-century humans!"

"That could change the whole course of history," said McMoo. "If humans discovered electro-beam weapons in 1066 they might have wiped themselves out by 1100!"

"Precisely," Daisy agreed. "So, using sign language, I did a deal with Bettie – if she kept my stuff a secret and gave me a place to hide while I tried to get the F.B.I. time machine working again, then I would do something nice for her in return. And once she clocked my dazzling Christmas decorations, she realized she could use them to get in with William the Conqueror."

Bo frowned. "How come?"

"William needed a lot of help to win over the people of England," Daisy confided. "But my dazzling decs proved just the job! Because of them, William is really popular. He'll be crowned king on Christmas Day, and he'll probably make Bettie a princess or something. Everyone's a winner!"

"That's a turn up," Bo remarked. "For once it's *not* the F.B.I. playing time tricks – it's the C.I.A.!"

"But where did so many decorations come from, Daisy?" asked Pat. "They can't *all* have come from your workshop?"

"Course they didn't, love!" Daisy leaned closer. "When I took the time machine to bits, I found enough electronic bits and pieces to build a *Short-Life Replicator*."

Bo blinked. "A Shortbread Reptile Butler?"

"A Short-Life Replicator. It makes a perfect copy of anything you stick inside it," Daisy explained. "But the copy only lasts a short time. All these baubles, lights and decorations will vanish away to nothing just after Christmas – so no naughty future technology can fall into anyone's hands!" She beamed. "You know, it's funny – I was trying to make a replicator back in 2550, it's a big top-secret project . . ."

"That's a remarkable coincidence," McMoo agreed, looking slightly awkward. "Well, I'm sorry I misjudged you, Daisy. You did what you had to do, and did it very cleverly. If the decorations won't last, no real harm has been done."

"Right," Daisy agreed. "Today is Christmas Eve, and tomorrow the conqueror will be crowned king!" She fluttered her eyelids at McMoo. "And now *you're* here, dearie, you can whisk me back to my own time!"

"I wish I could," said McMoo. "But right now my Time Shed is up the spout." He checked the long-range Time-Power Sensor. "The energy banks just aren't charging up properly."

"I've not got much power myself,"

Daisy confided. "My electro-beam sends energy through the air, but it isn't very strong. And after that blast I gave Ethelbad and his men, there's barely enough left to work the Christmas lights."

Bo smiled. "So *that's* how the decorations work without being plugged in!"

"The whole mystery is solved," said Pat happily. "Result!"

"I'm afraid not," said McMoo. "Not quite. There's still this business of Ethelbad's 'special' turkeys."

"As far as I'm concerned," said Bo, "Ethelbad can make like his turkeys and get stuffed!"

"You're missing the point," the professor told her. "Turkeys were first discovered in America. And America hasn't been discovered yet. Turkeys won't come to Europe for hundreds of years."

Bo scratched her head. "So the F.B.I.

are playing about with time . . ."

Pat nodded. "*And* working with Ethelbad."

Suddenly, the door slammed open – and Bettie Barmas appeared, her ugly face twisted in angry surprise. "*Oi!* What are you  three troublemakers doing in my house? Get away from my cow. Get out!"

Before Daisy could react, the burly woman grabbed McMoo and hurled him through the door, then dragged Bo and Pat out by the scruffs of their necks and sent them sprawling into a large rickety wagon parked in the street outside.

McMoo lay beside them, sniffing the air. "I can smell something . . ."

Bo pointed to the wagon, its contents concealed by a large dirty blanket. "The niff's coming from there, Professor."

"It's . . ." Pat gasped. "Sage and onion stuffing!"

"'Ere!" cried Bettie from the doorway. "Get away from my wagon. Clear off!"

But Bo snatched away the blanket — and the three cows gasped.

There, gleaming in the moonlight in the back of the wagon, was an enormous, teetering tower of oven-ready turkeys!

Chapter Eight

THE TURKEY OF TERROR

"It was you having that secret meeting with Ethelbad, wasn't it, Bettie?" McMoo looked gravely at the pile of poultry. "Everyone will think these turkeys come from William the Conqueror because you will be handing them out, just as you handed out all the decorations."

"So what?" growled Bettie, unloading the mountain of plucked birds into her house. "If that Saxon sausage-head wants to make William look good by giving out these big juicy birds, why should I stop him?"

"He said the turkeys had been 'prepared'," McMoo reminded her. "He might have poisoned them for all you know!"

"Rubbish!" Bettie heaved the last bird inside. "Now, mind your own business and push off!" She went inside and slammed the door behind her.

Daisy pressed her nose to the grimy window and mimed, "Sorry!" – then the shutter slammed closed.

"Is Bettie just being stupid?" Bo wondered. "Or is she up to something?"

"I'm not sure," murmured McMoo. "But if Ethelbad's working with the F.B.I., we must find out what he's up to."

"Meanwhile, let's warn William," said Pat. "If he tells everyone the turkeys *haven't* come from him, it will spoil Ethelbad's plans!"

"Good thinking," Bo declared.

"Yes, go and see him now, both of you," said McMoo. "Meanwhile, I'll keep an eye on Bettie and the turkeys. With Daisy's help perhaps we can get our hands on one of them." He winked at his young friends. "Good luck!"

Pat and Bo moved quickly through the snowy London streets. The star-scattered sky loomed dark and threatening overhead despite the flashing Christmas lights.

Soon, they reached the forest. But they hadn't got far through the wintry scrub and pines when they heard movement ahead of them.

"Uh-oh," Pat whispered, holding still.

"Who's there?" bellowed Bo fiercely. "Come out now – or be very, very sorry!"

"Calm yourself, *madame*!" came a familiar voice – and Renouf the Norman trotted out of the shadows on

83

his horse. "We don't want to be beaten up!"

"No indeed," added Tostain, appearing just behind him. "We are merely patrolling these woods for naughty Saxons."

Renouf nodded. "We wondered whether Lord Angus had dealt with Ethelbad and set you free – and clearly he has!"

"It's not quite as simple as that," Pat sighed. "Ethelbad is causing trouble that only William can deal with. The crown of England may be at stake! We must speak with the conqueror right away."

"William is asleep," said Renouf. "He ate a midnight supper of pilchards in brandy and will not be disturbed."

"Not very fair," Pat remarked, "when his bum will be disturbing the whole camp after a late-night snack like that!"

"True," said Tostain ruefully. "But pilchards are his favourites."

"Must be why he hangs around with you two," said Bo, hopping up and down impatiently. "Stop wasting time and let's go and see him – *now*!"

McMoo spent the whole night huddled up in his cloak, braving the Christmas cold down an alley close to Bettie's house. Finally, at about six in the morning, the wooden door was unbolted and Bettie lumbered out with an armful of turkeys.

"Uh-oh," murmured McMoo, as she bunged the birds back onto her wagon. "She must be off to make her first delivery . . ."

While Bettie kept on loading, McMoo crept up to the other side of the cart

and fiddled with
one of the
wheels so it
became loose.
Then he
sneaked away
again.

As Bettie
perched the last turkey on top of the
pile and tried to heave the wagon away,
the wheel fell off with a splintering
crack and the turkeys spilled into the
street. McMoo chortled to himself, his
sabotage a success.

But the massive woman simply marched up to the house next door and banged hard on the door. "Oi, Wulnoth! Can I borrow your cart?"

"S'pose. It's parked round the back," came the gruff, sleepy answer.

"Typical," McMoo muttered, as he scuttled back over to the wagon. This time he snatched up a turkey and ran away with it.

Bettie came back seconds later with another wagon and threw the birds onto it. Then, with the strength of a shire horse, she dragged the wagon away,

ready to deliver the special turkeys to the noble families of old London.

As soon as she was out of sight, McMoo carried his catch over to Bettie's house and knocked on the door.

Daisy threw it open with relief. "Oh, Angus, come in, you poor mite," she fussed. "Thank goodness you got a turkey! I tried to take one for you, but Bettie went to sleep on top of the pile. Wriggling about on them all night, she was . . ."

McMoo grimaced. "I hope she was wearing a nightie!" He quickly placed the trussed-up turkey on Daisy's workbench. "Now, how can we test this thing?"

"If it's poisoned, perhaps it will smell funny when it's cooked," Daisy suggested. "Folk in this time wouldn't know the difference."

"Good point," said McMoo. "Let's use your electro-beam to cook a bit."

"Cows roasting turkeys — it's not right," Daisy muttered as she fiddled with her torch-like gadget. "Still, for you, Angus, my sweet, I'll give it a go."

The electro-beam hummed loudly,

and the cows were soon holding their noses as the whiff of cooked turkey began to fill the little house.

Then suddenly, the oven-ready animal twitched!

"Aaagh!" Daisy shrieked. "It's not dead!"

"Of course it is," McMoo retorted, staring in alarm as the turkey started to shake. "It's been stuffed, it's—"

"*Alive!*" yelled Daisy, as the plucked bird suddenly turned inside out in a shower of sage and onion stuffing – to reveal a robotic turkey! A silver head slid out from the chunky metal frame. Two yellow eyes fixed on the professor, and the creature shook out a pair of metal wings,

its dagger-sharp beak quivering.

"Bless my buttercups," breathed
McMoo. "It's a cyber-turkey!"

And with an eerie, electronic gobbling
noise, the chunky metal monster
pounced on him, dragging him to
the floor!

"Oof!" McMoo gasped, desperately
fending off the computerized poultry.
It pecked at him wildly, its terrifying
talons poised to rake his hide. "Daisy,
help me! The electro-beam . . ." The
flustered cow grabbed the gadget and
smashed it down on the cyber-turkey's

silver skull! With a flash of sparks and a clatter of wings, the menacing bird-bot flapped backwards and dropped to the ground.

"Thanks," said McMoo weakly. "I actually meant for you to send a high-intensity electrostatic blast into its central processing unit – but conking it on the head was good too!" He scrambled back up. "This must be one of the sneakiest F.B.I. plots yet. A stealth-robot in turkey trousers – activated by heat!"

Daisy gasped. "Bettie's handing them out to the most noble families in London, ready to be cooked tomorrow. As soon as those birds feel the heat of the fire . . ."

"Hey presto!" McMoo concluded. "They turn into turkey-assassins."

"And then everyone turns against William the Conqueror despite all my work with those darling decorations. If they refuse to crown him, history will be changed — and the F.B.I. can start to take control of a different future." Daisy glowered down at the techno-turkey. "We need to stop Bettie handing them out!"

"She refused to listen last time," sighed McMoo. "I think we should go after Ethelbad."

"Must we?" Daisy pulled a face. "He gives me the willies."

"But he gave Bettie the *turkeys*! And if we get him, perhaps we can stop this problem at its source." The professor grabbed the dented metal bird and a screwdriver. "First, let's make sure this thing is really taken care of. Then, whatever the risks, we have to find Ethelbad and stop him — before Christmas Day becomes Deadly Turkeys-of-Doom Day, and all future history gets flushed down the toilet!"

Chapter Nine

MOOSTAKEN IDENTITY

"I've had enough of this!" cried Bo. "How much longer do we have to wait?"

Pat gave his sister a warning look. True enough, they had been waiting in the snow outside William the Conqueror's private tent for hours now. Despite Renouf and Tostain's best efforts, the six enormous bodyguards refused to let them pass. Bo's complaints were falling on deaf ears – and Pat was worried that soon they would fall on very sharp swords . . .

"I'm sure he'll be awake in a minute," said Tostain, for about the hundredth time.

Then Pat had an idea. "Wow, look over there!" he called loudly. "An extra-big delivery of pilchards has just come in!"

In a flash, the flap to William's tent opened and the man himself burst out in his nightgown. "Pilchards?" the conqueror demanded, sniffing the air. "Where? Where?"

"Um, there are no pilchards, your grace," said Pat, trying to hold his voice steady. "That was only a ruse."

"A ruse, eh?" William looked blank. "Does a ruse *taste* like a pilchard?"

"Oi! Newsflash for Billy the Conk!" Bo shouted. "You've got bigger fish to fry than pilchards – *turkeys!*"

"Turkeys aren't fish," Pat reminded her.

"True," Bo agreed, "but there *is* something fishy about these turkeys!"

"If they're fishy then I'm interested," said William happily. "Tell me your news!"

"OK," said Pat, with a nervous glance at Bo. "Here goes . . ."

Having taken the bashed-in techno-turkey apart and rewired its insides, McMoo and Daisy walked nervously through the winding streets towards Ethelbad's domain.

But when they arrived, the Saxon's stinky stronghold was deserted.

"Where is everyone?" wondered Daisy.

"Good question," said McMoo, peering around cautiously. "Wish I had a good answer . . ."

"Try this one." The lumpy figure of

Bettie Barmas strode out from the rotting hall in the middle of the camp. "He's over at Westminster Abbey, rehearsing his coronation!"

"His *what*? Oh, no, hang on . . ." McMoo stared at her empty wagon in horror. "Don't tell me you've delivered all those turkeys already?"

"Course I have," Bettie shrugged. "It's Christmas tomorrow – people will be cooking them in the morning."

"But they mustn't!" McMoo waved his deactivated techno-turkey. "This is one Christmas dinner that bites back!"

Daisy nodded. "Those things are heat-activated robotic killers in disguise. Everybody must be warned!"

"You're not wearing a ringblender, Daisy," McMoo reminded her. "She doesn't understand you."

"Oh, but I *do*, Professor," said Bettie quietly. "It's *you* who doesn't understand."

"What?" McMoo frowned. "How did you know I'm a professor?"

"The same way I can understand the cow language spoken by dear Daisy Micklepud there. As well as old Norman and Saxon and any other language in the world." Bettie gave them both a horrible smile and her voice suddenly turned into a metallic drone. "Because *I AM A TER-MOO-NATOR!*"

McMoo and Daisy stared in shock as the woman began to peel away her face. It was only a mask . . . !

"Oh, no." McMoo groaned. "I should have realized!"

Bettie's Saxon dress dropped to the ground to reveal a tough, grey hide half-hidden by metal armour. Her real face was part bull, part terrifying robot. It had eyes that glowed green, a grille for a mouth and a blazing red snout.

"I am Ter-moo-nator T-2512," declared the robo-bull in its grating voice. "But you may call me by my codename – Moodolph!"

"Moodolph the red-nosed ter-moo-nator." McMoo glowered at him. "Well, you're a clever one, Moodolph, I'll say that much. You knew C.I.A. agents would see through a ringblender – so you put on human fancy dress, swallowed a voice changer and disguised yourself as a woman!"

"The real Bettie Barmas is away visiting family in the country," Moodolph revealed. "Impersonating her has served me well. I was able to use her house as a base in this time, and I could walk about your farm without arousing suspicion."

"Of course," groaned McMoo. "It was *you* who left the booby-trapped present that sent us here. Just before the shed was attacked, we heard Bessie saying she couldn't be in two places at once – but with you around, she could!"

Daisy glared furiously at Moodolph. "You tricked me into thinking you were nice. Well, now I'll show you!" She charged at the robotic bull – but his red nose glowed brighter . . .

"No, Daisy!" McMoo frantically hurled himself at the angry cow and knocked her down – just as a laser beam fired from Moodolph's snout. It whizzed past Daisy's head and turned a tent into ashes. McMoo quickly dragged her behind another tent for cover.

"I tricked you from the start, milk cow!" sneered Moodolph, his nose smoking. "Our 'broken' time machine was rigged to bring you to 1066 – so you could serve the F.B.I.!" He sniggered. "Why arouse C.I.A. suspicions by stealing your work on the Short-Life Replicator when we could get you to finish your creation right here?"

"So it wasn't just luck that I had all the equipment I needed in your silly machine," Daisy realized.

"Of course not!" Moodolph advanced on their hiding place. "The F.B.I. built just one ter-moo-turkey. But thanks to your replicator, we now have loads!" He fired his nose-blaster again. McMoo and Daisy were thrown backwards as another tent exploded.

"Your clever little plot is going to backfire," shouted McMoo, joining Daisy behind a pile of smelly rubbish. "William the Conqueror's on his way. He'll tell everyone the turkeys came from Ethelbad, not him!"

"The ter-moo-turkeys are only *part* of my plan." Moodolph narrowed his eyes. "You believe that you arrived here by chance, Professor. But the holly-bat fused your Time Shed's controls. You would have ended up here no matter what you tried to do."

"Oh." McMoo sighed. "And I thought I was being so clever too!"

"Why *did* you bring him here?" Daisy demanded.

"Your electro-beam has limited power." Moodolph pulled out a small hand-held device. "And for the F.B.I. plan to succeed, we need more energy . . ."

"Energy that you're draining from the Time Shed's engines!" McMoo angrily checked his long-range Time-Power Sensor again – and found the display still blinking near empty. "No wonder the energy banks haven't been recharging. But what do you need extra power for?"

Moodolph smiled. "For *this*."

He pressed a button on his gadget. Professor McMoo heard a slithering noise behind him and whirled round . . .

To find a string of Christmas lights
rearing up like a poisonous snake!
Suddenly, it coiled itself around the
two cows.

Daisy shrieked as the green plastic
cord tightened about her tummy.
And the next moment, two illuminated
candy canes swooped down from the
sky and started beating McMoo over
the head!

"William's attempts to warn the people will fail. I shall simply bring forward my plans." Moodolph laughed. "You see, Daisy, while you slept I used your tools to turn your festive decorations into deadly weapons. Thanks to your replicator machine, they now hang all over London – ready to attack. What is more, the cyber-turkeys do not require fire to be activated." The robo-bull waved his little device. "I can send a heat impulse from this – and the chaos will be complete!"

"The deadly decs will terrify the common people, while the turkeys nobble the noble families – eliminating all other possible rulers." McMoo gasped as the candy canes conked him again. "Those who survive will have no choice but to follow Ethelbad!"

"Ethelbad will drive all Normans from England," hissed Moodolph. "And once he is made king, F.B.I. agents shall become his royal advisors. We shall ensure that Saxons stay simple and stupid, while cows are taught to wage war on their human masters. History shall be changed for ever, and cruel cattle will take over the world . . ."

"Never!" vowed McMoo. "The C.I.A. will stop you!"

"They have no idea what is happening here," jeered Moodolph. "Their time-scanners are designed to detect build-ups of F.B.I. activity – not transmissions from their own technology." He laughed as the fairy lights wrapped themselves ever tighter around Daisy and McMoo. "What a Christmas present for the F.B.I.! War-like cattle will rule for ever more – *and it is C.I.A. agents who have made it possible!*"

Chapter Ten

FESTIVE FURY

Pat and Bo travelled into London with the Norman army. Tostain walked behind them and Renouf rode upon his spotty horse as usual. William was also on horseback, trotting along grandly at the head of the procession, waving at people as he passed. But at the sight of so many soldiers, most Saxons hurried into their houses.

"I mean you no harm!" William cried, speaking not-very-good Anglo-Saxon. "Spread the word – the turkeys are not mine. I have never seen a turkey before! Honestly, I much prefer pilchards ..."

"I'm glad William believed our story," said Pat.

"I'm not so sure he does," Bo replied. "But with his coronation tomorrow, he's not taking any chances."

A Saxon maid shrieked as William and his soldiers marched round the corner towards Westminster Abbey. Washerwomen hurled their buckets into the air as they fled with their children. Merchants swiftly packed away their goods, and even beggars shuffled out of sight.

"Stand still, you silly people!" William commanded. "My men are not here to chop you into bits or fire arrows at you – I'm bored with all that nonsense . . ."

"It's no good," said Renouf, dismayed. "They're too scared to listen to anything the duke says!"

"I'm nice! I'm a good guy!" William insisted. "Why else would I give you such lovely Christmas decorations?"

But even as he spoke, a holly wreath hanging on a nearby door started to twitch. So did a piece of tinsel, nailed to the house next door.

"That's weird," said Bo. The fairy lights dangling from the thatched rooftops began to shake and swing of their own accord and the bulbs burned brighter and brighter . . .

Then suddenly, the decorations attacked!

Candy canes burst from the walls and tree baubles streamed out of the sky. The wreaths erupted into bat-like bits of holly, flapping madly through the narrow streets.

"Hit the deck!" Pat shouted, diving to the snowy ground.

"I can't!" Bo yelped as a candy cane cracked her on the head and a bunch of baubles bashed into her belly. "The decs are hitting me! Ow!"

William's horse reared up in alarm and his soldiers started to panic when ropes of tinsel came slithering down the street like glittering snakes. "What witchcraft is this?" cried the conqueror. "What has become of my delectable decorations?"

"That's what I'd like to know!" Pat gasped, as the vicious holly-bats hurtled about him. "Have you noticed, Bo? They're only after you and me!"

"They attack the Saxons in the street as well," Tostain observed. He drew his bow and arrow and shot a candy cane

in two – but the next moment, an identical one whizzed up to attack Bo instead. "There's no stopping the things!"

"Let's get indoors out of sight," Pat yelled over the clamour of screaming Saxons. He staggered to the nearest door and battered it with his hooves. It swung open – and a blizzard of baubles swept out from the house, bashing him all over! "*Help!*"

Renouf hopped off his horse and helped Tostain kick the baubles away from Pat. Then Bo dragged him under Renouf's trusty horse for shelter.

"That holly's like the thing that stuffed up the Time Shed," she realized. "The F.B.I. must be behind this attack too!"

"Right." Pat nodded, panting for breath. "They've outsmarted us, Bo. It's not just the turkeys they've tampered with. Everything William has touched is now turning on the people – so the people will turn on *him*!"

Back in Ethelbad's camp, the sounds of Saxon panic carried eerily from the London streets.

"Hear that?" Moodolph the ter-moo-nator sniggered. "The cow's decorations are attacking the population."

"Oh, Angus!" Daisy sobbed, flinging her arms around his neck.

"Steady," gasped McMoo, clawing at the ever-tightening cord of Christmas tree lights crushing his chest. "You're strangling me faster than these things!"

"Looks like our goose is cooked," said Daisy, "even if those terrible turkeys aren't!"

"How glorious it is to change history," rasped Moodolph.

McMoo glared at him defiantly. "You're . . . crazy!"

"And you are doomed," said

Moodolph with satisfaction. "Now, I must make sure that Ethelbad does not bungle his big moment." Moodolph unfolded a monk's cowl from a compartment in his metal leg, put it on as a disguise, then turned and strode away. "Farewell, fools!"

"I thought he'd never leave," groaned McMoo. Then he whistled, as if summoning a dog. "Here, Rover! Come to Daddy!"

The deactivated cyber-turkey switched itself on at his command and rose shakily to its evil clawed-feet.

"Looks like our changes to its control centre paid off," squeaked Daisy.

"Don't count your chickens – or your turkeys – before they've hatched!" McMoo winced as the possessed plastic cord grew tighter still. "We don't know for sure Rover is on our side." He managed another whistle. "Here, boy! Set us free!"

The robo-
turkey
hesitated.
Then it
wobbled
over and set
about the
fairy lights. It
pecked at the
plastic with its nail-sharp beak and tore
off the bulbs with its terrible talons.
Soon the C.I.A. agents were free.

"Well done, my little poppet!" said
Daisy, blowing Rover a kiss.

"Daisy, please!" McMoo protested.
"Talking to turkeys is considered one of
the first signs of madness." He paused.
"Isn't it, Rover?"

The cyber-turkey gave a wobbly
gobble.

"Thought so," the professor sighed.
"We *must* be mad to think we can
stop Moodolph, Ethelbad, a city full

of deadly decorations and a few dozen killer-turkeys all at once . . ."

Daisy nodded. "No power on Earth could stop that lot."

"Power?" McMoo stared at her. "That's it – *power*! Moodolph's barmy army of festive things is running on energy from your electro-beam and my Time Shed."

"And if we can stop them getting that power," Daisy realized, "then the F.B.I. plan will grind to a halt!"

"So what are we waiting for – Christmas?" McMoo gave her a wild grin, grabbed Rover and sprinted from Ethelbad's camp. "Let's go!"

Still beating back bloodthirsty baubles and killer candy canes, Pat, Bo and their Norman friends had struggled through the panic-stricken Saxon streets and were close to Westminster Abbey. High above, the holly-bats were hurling down bright-red berry bombs that splattered stinging juice everywhere.

"Come!" William commanded his friends, galloping down the street towards the ornate stone building. "I shall open the abbey doors, so that the people may hide inside. Its sturdy walls will offer shelter to those who need it."

"Wanna bet?" boomed an unpleasant but familiar voice.

"Oh, no," groaned Pat, as the Normans skidded to a halt.

Bo scowled. "He's all we need."

Ethelbad and his burly band were blocking the way. A gloating, gap-toothed grin sat upon the Saxon chief's face. "No Norman ninnies may set foot in my abbey!"

"*Your* abbey?" Bo frowned.

He nodded. "My men and I have just done it up with the finest stuffed rats and cabbage flowers – ready for my crowning moment tomorrow!"

As Ethelbad spoke, Pat saw that the square outside Westminster Abbey was filling up with frightened Saxons chased by baubles, candy canes and hissing fairy lights. Suddenly, the big man swung round to address them.

"Hear me, people of London," he bellowed. "You are being punished by the spirit of Christmas itself! Punished because you were ready to accept the gifts of William the Conqueror.

Punished because you were ready to
accept him as your king! Punished
because you would not follow *me*!"

"Rubbish!" Bo shouted. She tried to
blow a raspberry, but a cheeky length of
tinsel gagged her before she could.

"The Norman decorations are
bewitched!" Ethelbad went on. "They
turn against you for trusting the
invaders." More strings of fairy lights
were wriggling in sinister snake-like

fashion towards the square – and yet they ignored Ethelbad and his men completely. "See? William's naughty gifts dare not harm me, nor those who follow me. It is the fates' way of saying that I, Ethelbad the 'Orrible, must become King of England – and only those who follow me shall be saved!"

"He's right!" gasped a washerwoman, held tight by fairy lights.

"We must follow Ethelbad!" cried a little old man, hopping about with a bauble up his trouser leg. "We must!"

"No, you *mustn't*!" shouted William. "Guards – shut the smelly Saxon up!"

William's men drew their swords. Ethelbad's men drew theirs. For a few moments, the two groups stood there yelling noisily and making rude signals at each other.

Then William yelled at the top of his voice: "Let battle commence!"

Chapter Eleven

COW-ER FROM THE POWER

Renouf charged bravely towards the band of burly Saxons, Tostain and the other Norman knights at his heels. A pitched battle broke out! William joined in the fighting, swapping sword-blows with Ethelbad.

"Your grace, no! Don't fight the Saxons!" Pat yelled, batting away a hovering candy cane. "You must help protect the people from those evil decorations!"

"There is nothing anyone can do for them now," said a cold, grating voice close by.

With a thrill of alarm, Pat noticed the cloaked figure of a monk standing close by the abbey doors – and glimpsed glowing green eyes inside the cowl. "Oh, no, Bo, look!" he cried. "It's a ter-moo-nator!"

"Where?" Bo gasped, trying to see past a length of angry tinsel. "I'll get him in a minute!"

"Don't think so," said the ter-moo-nator, as a barrage of baubles banged into Bo's bottom, knocking her over. "I, Moodolph, have defeated you utterly!"

The tinsel whipped itself around Bo's waist and pulled tight. Pat fought to free her, but hundreds more plastic candy canes rained down on him like truncheons.

He covered his aching head.

Close by, metal clanged on metal as Ethelbad, William and their forces fought ever more fiercely . . .

"Face it, C.I.A. fools," Moodolph gloated. "This is a battle you will never win."

"Want to bet?" came a familiar cry.

The fighting stopped for a second. "Look!" bellowed William in delight, pointing across the square. "Lord Angus of Burger!"

Tostain frowned. "And he's brought a performing cow with him!"

Pat stared in amazement as Professor McMoo and Daisy charged across the crowded square pursued by holly-bats, candy canes and a whole bauble battalion. Daisy held the electro-beam high above her head, her hooves fiddling with the controls.

"Remember how she used that thing to save us in that alley, Pat?" said Bo excitedly. "I think she's going to do it again—"

Ga-bammmm! Bo whooped as the tinsel that held her burst into sparks and then withered to nothing.

The candy canes attacking Pat flew up in the air and exploded. The baubles fell to the ground and bounced wildly about like glowing tennis balls.

"That was the last of the electro-beam's power!" Daisy yelled.

"The energy burn-out has destroyed all

decorations in the local area," Moodolph observed coldly.

McMoo beamed. "That was the idea, tin-head!" He and Daisy waded through the stunned Saxons and Normans around them to reach Pat and Bo. "Hello, you two. Having a happy Christmas so far?"

"It's different," Pat admitted.

"Listen closely." McMoo lowered his voice. "That pile of tinned steak over there is now running his deadly decs purely on energy stolen from the Time Shed. He will soon be bringing out reinforcements – we *have* to cut his power supply. Daisy knows what to do, but she will need backup."

"I'll go with her, Prof," Bo volunteered. "Renouf, can I borrow your horse?"

Renouf jumped down from his horse and bowed. "As you wish, my lady."

"And I'll have yours, chuck," Daisy told William – although to his ears it sounded like "*MOOOOOO!*"

William stared in shock as the cow
leaped onto his proud stallion and
almost squashed it. But then the horse
recovered and carried Daisy away after
Bo through the snowy, slippery streets.

"You should have run with your milk-
cow friends, Professor," hissed Moodolph.
"Your interference has achieved nothing.
In fact, I shall turn it to my advantage."
So saying, he turned to address the
Saxon crowds. "Behold, the demon
decorations are destroyed! It is as mighty
Ethelbad said – those who have sworn
to follow him are protected from the

vile Normans' wizardry, just as he is!"

"That weirdo monk is right!" shouted the old man, broken baubles now tumbling from out of his trouser legs.

"No!" yelled McMoo desperately. "Don't believe him!"

"How can we not?" The washerwoman raised a broom like a pikestaff. "We promised to follow him, and the witchcraft ended. Let us fight for Ethelbad, our true king!"

"*AT LAST!*" bellowed Ethelbad, bearing down on William as his Saxon band resumed battle with glee. "The people follow me. They are mine to command – and I command them to *DESTROY YOU ALL!*"

"*WAIT!*" hollered McMoo at the top of his lungs.

Pat held his ears. Compelled by the command in the professor's voice, everyone stood still for a moment – even Ethelbad and Moodolph.

McMoo addressed the mob of Saxons in the square. "The wizardry you have witnessed was not caused by William, and Bettie Barmas had nothing to do with it either. Ethelbad is responsible — and he is *not* protected. The proof's right here." He pulled Rover the cyber-turkey from under his cloak and chucked him at Ethelbad. "Rover — sort the bad man out!"

With an electronic squawk, the bird-bot flapped dizzily through the air and crashed into the Saxon chief. "Ooof!" gasped Ethelbad, toppling under the impact. "Gerroff!"

"Bad turkey!" hissed Moodolph, trying to grab hold of the silver bird while slipping in the snow. "Stop!" But Rover pecked at the ter-moo-nator's robes and tore them away — revealing Moodolph in all his half-bull, half-robot glory. The ter-moo-nator tripped over his clothes and fell down. With a victorious

squawk, the cyber-turkey sat on his
head and leaked oil all over him.

"Flying metal birds!" screamed a
woman in the crowd.

"Talking monk-bulls in shiny
armour!" moaned another, fainting.

Soon, hundreds more were shrieking
and running away from this latest
assault on their sanity.

"No!" Ethelbad staggered up,
horrified. "My people! Don't leave your
leader – come back!" Desperately he
ran after the fleeing crowds. His baffled
band of men shrugged and followed.

"Chickens!" William yelled after them.

Tostain smiled. "You mean 'turkeys', your grace."

"You shall pay for your meddling, Professor!" grated Moodolph, finally trapping the rogue turkey beneath one of his solid steel hooves. "I *had* planned to attack only the would-be leaders of London with the cyber-turkeys. But now, using the power of your Time Shed, I shall activate them and destroy you, your friends and hundreds of those innocent Saxons you seem to care so much about. *Then* I shall make it seem as though Ethelbad has defeated them. The survivors of this attack will hail him as a hero."

Pat bit his lip. "And with William out of the way, Ethelbad will be the only choice for the new King of England."

"You see? The future *still* belongs to the F.B.I.!" Moodolph's voice rose to a metallic shriek as he activated his remote control. "*Nothing* can stop us now!"

In fine homes all over London, the freshly delivered cyber-turkeys picked up Moodolph's signal and burst into sudden, uncanny life. Sage and onion stuffing sprayed the wooden walls as the apparently innocent birds turned inside out, revealing their true deadly forms.

People fled through the snowy streets in fear – but there was no escape. The remaining candy canes, holly-bats and baubles began to herd the Saxons towards the ter-moo-turkeys. Tinsel snakes joined in, tripping and tangling up their victims, holding them helpless as the robotic poultry advanced . . .

"Have no fear, my people!" hollered Ethelbad. "I will save you all!" He smiled. "Er, when my friend the metal bull tells me how to, that is . . ."

129

"Stop this, Moodolph!" cried McMoo, as a squadron of ter-moo-turkeys landed with a squawk in the square and surrounded them. "Call off the attack."

"Why should I?" the ter-moo-nator enquired.

"Er . . . Because it's Christmas!" Pat shouted. "The season of goodwill!"

"Yes – and it *will* be *good* to squish you," Moodolph retorted.

William the Conqueror was still looking bewildered. "The talking bull sends silver birds to do battle with men?"

"Fear not! Renouf shouted, drawing his sword, "I shall deal with our trifling foes . . ." But the nearest cyber-turkey pecked his weapon in two with a single swipe of its beak. "Or not," Renouf concluded weakly, falling back beside Tostain.

"I just hope Bo and Daisy cut the power in time," muttered Pat.

"What?" Moodolph overheard and frowned sharply. "Where did you send the milk-cows, Professor? To cut the power in time?"

"No, no! To cut some *parsley and thyme*!" said McMoo desperately. "They fancied a grass sandwich, and—"

"They've gone to the Time Shed to cut the power link, haven't they," Moodolph realized, his nose glowing crimson with fury. "Well, we'll see about that!" He leaped into the air – and jets in his hooves propelled him up and away into the sky. He streaked off into the distance.

William went cross-eyed, then fell over in the snow. And the menacing turkeys stalked ever closer.

"We must try to hold out against these birds for as long as we can," McMoo told Renouf, Tostain and the others. "Bo and, er, the circus-cow may still be in time to save us!"

"Cows on horseback outrunning a supersonic ter-moo-nator?" Pat sighed helplessly. "We haven't a hope!"

Chapter Twelve

THE SQUIRTS THAT SAVED CHRISTMOOS

Bo drove her struggling horse on, faster and faster through the forest, with Daisy just keeping up beside her. "When we reach the shed, what are we looking for?" she called. "A dirty big cable plugged into the wall stretching all the way back to the ter–moo–nator's house?"

"No, it will be a wireless connection," Daisy shouted back over the rush of the wind in their ears. "Looks like a bright orange ball of energy."

"You will never reach it!" came a grating groan from above them.

"Moodolph's on our trail," said Bo grimly. The next moment, a red laser beam blew up a bush close by! "Come on, Daisy, keep going. We *must* keep going!"

Weaving in and out of Moodolph's laser bolts, the cows galloped over the top of a hill.

"There's the Time Shed!" Bo cried. "Come on, just a little further!"

Desperately, the two cows rode the final few hundred metres to reach the battered old building. Bo could see a glowing orange ball, sparking with weird energy just beside the door.

"That's what I've got to switch off," said Daisy, jumping down from her exhausted horse.

But then, Moodolph swooped down from the sky and landed just in front of them – blocking their way.

"No!" Bo shouted.

"Now you cannot reach the power interface," rasped Moodolph. "And I shall ter-moo-nate you."

"Shut it, steak-breath." Bo leaped from her stallion. "We don't have to reach your stupid power interface to sort it out – because we've got something you don't. *Milk-cow* power."

Daisy grinned as she got Bo's meaning. "That should do the trick . . ."

Moodolph's nose turned dark red as he powered it up for a mega-blast. "Prepare to die!"

"Prepare for a double milkshake!" Bo shouted back, hitching up her skirts. "Cows in Action – *hi-yaaa!*"

An enormous squoosh of milk burst from both cows' udders, jetting past Moodolph's shoulders and showering the power interface. The glowing orange ball crackled and sizzled, and black smoke swirled out from inside it.

"No!" Moodolph swung round in alarm to see. But his over-charged nose could no longer contain its laser energy. It burst out in a red, sparking torrent – and blew up the interface!

"Ha!" squealed Daisy, hopping up and down with glee. "The C.I.A. might have made your plan possible – but in the end it was *you* who stopped it!"

"*Noooooooooooo!*" Moodolph warbled.

"Come on, Daisy, let's squirt him too!" laughed Bo.

The ter-moo-nator glubbed and snorted as the cows' milk sprayed and sizzled over his circuits. "Mission abort!" He fumbled for his portable time machine, a silver disk hidden behind his

chest plate. "Unhappy Christmas!
Mission abort . . ."

He clanked onto the disk and
disappeared in a puff of green and
red smoke . . .

Pat braced himself while the
surrounding ter-moo-turkeys prepared
to pounce. Renouf tried to defend
Tostain with his broken sword. Professor
McMoo backed away as an evil beak
opened wide . . .

But then suddenly, the turkey about
to nip him went cross-eyed and flew
backwards. It smashed into two more of

the metal monsters, sending electric shocks through them. They jumped and gobbled in electronic surprise, flapping about in circles.

"What's happening?" asked Tostain in a daze.

"Run!" McMoo commanded. "While they're distracted . . ."

But Pat saw the street beyond was alive with coils of fairy lights and tinsel, slithering through the snow towards them. "It's too late!"

"Never say die, Pat," McMoo told him – then smiled as the fairy lights began to smoke, and the snow started to boil around them. "Try saying, 'energy feedback from the power interface is destroying the F.B.I.'s Christmas killers' instead. It's much more fun!"

Pat stared around in amazement. The electronic turkeys were falling to bits. Candy canes were plummeting from the sky and shattering. Baubles bumped together and broke apart, and the holly-bats simply blinked out of existence with a thousand high-pitched *pops*.

"They did it . . ." Pat smiled. "Bo and Daisy – somehow, they did it!"

"They scrambled the power supply," McMoo agreed happily, as all the fairy lights faded away. "And the energy surge has caused Daisy's Short-Life Replicas to vanish a little earlier than Moodolph would have liked."

"Then there will be just one of each of the decorations left behind," Pat realized.

McMoo nodded. "And one cyber-turkey too. Much easier to clean up." He crossed to where a limp, silver figure lay on the snowy ground, and scooped it up. "And how do you like that – Rover must have been the real one! With a bit of tinkering he'll be as good as new and still on our side."

The robot gave him a wonky wink.

"Look!" Renouf pointed across the square, which was starting to fill up with bewildered Saxons. "There's quite a crowd coming."

Tostain crouched beside William the Conqueror. "Wake up, your grace. Quick!"

"The menace of the deadly decorations is over!" McMoo proclaimed to the people. "The 'orrible Ethelbad was behind everything – but Duke William here has put things right!"

"What's that?" said William, dizzily trying to stand. "Oh, yes, that's right. Of course I did!"

"Hail our new king!" someone shouted, and soon many others were joining in.

"No!" wailed Ethelbad, pushing through the crowd with his men, red-faced and worn out. "It's not fair. Everything's gone wrong! I was going to rule – whoops!" He tripped up, and his helmet fell off – to reveal a shiny pink patch on top of his head.

"Ethelbad!" someone laughed. "Ethel*bald*, more like!"

"Push off, smelly!" shouted someone else, and soon the whole crowd was booing Ethelbad and his followers.

"I shall drive these bullying upstarts from the city for you, my friends!" shouted William. "Come, Renouf! Come, Tostain! Come, all!"

With a rousing cheer, the Norman knights charged after their master. The Saxon crowds applauded, and Ethelbad's men turned on their heels and ran for it. Seeing his cause was lost, Ethelbad finally gave up and ran away too.

"That's good." McMoo smiled. "William seems to be back in favour! He will get his crown, and England will get a new start." The professor steered Pat away down the slushy, decoration-free streets. "And we had better make a start too — on all the repairs the Time Shed's going to need!"

Pat and Bo stopped off at Bettie Barmas's house and fixed her wagon. Then they loaded Daisy's workbench and all her other future things onto the back of it. Pat jumped on top. McMoo tugged his ringblender from his nose and got busy pulling the cart like a true bull.

"I hope the real Bettie won't get into trouble for handing out those dodgy decorations," said Pat.

"I'm sure William will give her a royal pardon," said McMoo. "In any case, built like that I think she's more than able to take care of herself!"

Forty minutes later they had reached the Time Shed. Bo ran up and hugged them both, and they all swapped stories. Daisy, meanwhile, used all her electrical skills on the Time Shed's broken systems.

"Old Moodolph sucked out a lot of power," she reported. "But there's just enough to jump-start her and drive back to 2550 for repairs."

Pat blinked. "How on Earth do you jump-start a shed?"

"Simple," said McMoo. "I'll just let a little of that lighter-than-air time-power leak out like I did before." He waggled his cyber-turkey. "And once we're up in the air, good old Rover here can give us a tow!"

"I'll rig up a force-field so you can

144

steer the little turkey trooper from the roof," Daisy offered.

"Brilliant!" cried McMoo, shinning up the side of the shed. "Let's get going!"

Pat and Bo unloaded the wagon, McMoo and Daisy did their bits of repairs, and by nightfall they were ready to go. McMoo had rigged up a harness for Rover, and was wearing his Santa hat to keep warm up on the roof.

"I just thought of something," said Pat suddenly. "Bo, what happens every Christmas Eve?"

Bo shrugged. "Farmer Christmoos flies through the night sky on top of a big barn pulled by turkeys, delivering presents to farm animals all over the world . . ." She gasped and looked up at McMoo. "Professor, you look just like him!"

"Blimey, you're right!" said Daisy. "What if a certain bull is watching when we take off? What if that's where

the real Farmer Christmoos gets the
idea from?"

Pat gulped. "That will mean we've
changed history!"

"Oh, 'changed' is a bit strong," said
McMoo, grinning. "Let's think of it as us
leaving history – and all the farmyard
animals to come – a little Christmas
present . . . But not a word to Yak!" He
winked down at his friends. "*Giddy up,
Rover . . .*"

"Are we off?" asked Bo.

"No time like the present." McMoo sighed happily. "And no present like the *Christmas* present. Merry Christmoos, everyone!"

"Merry Christmoos!" cheered the others.

Daisy, Bo and Pat went inside, and Rover began to flap his metal wings. The Time Shed rose slowly into the air, and the cyber-turkey towed it away into the night sky, his metal bits and pieces jingling like sleigh bells.

"Woo-hooooo!" McMoo cheered, his Santa hat billowing in the wintry breeze.

Higher and faster they went, soaring way above the quiet, snowy fields and hillsides of William's new land. Then the engines kicked in properly, the Time Shed glowed like a magical shooting star, and slowly faded from sight . . . carrying the Cows in Action from Christmas long-ago into the sparkling, festive future.

THE END